TRAVELLERS'
TALES

Peter Porter
Jan 89

Travellers' Tales

PETER RUSH

Illustrated by Peter Rush

Kaye & Ward : Kingswood

First published by Kaye & Ward Limited, The Windmill Press, Kingswood,
Tadworth, Surrey 1983

ISBN 0 7182 5085 0

Filmset in Baskerville by Filmtype Services Limited, Scarborough, North Yorkshire.
Printed in England by
Biddles Ltd, Guildford and King's Lynn

For J and for Thistle, Bill, Oliva,
Sinjin and Thomas

Travellers' Tales

The frozen winter landscape outside the scullery window looked quiet and still. The yard and the woods behind and the fields beyond those seemed like a landscape from a television screen. Cold, and a colourless grey-blue.

Percy, aged eight years (nine nearly), turned back from the window where he had rubbed himself a peep-hole in the moisture and looked round the farmhouse kitchen; at his uncle, asleep by the fire, and his aunt reading the Sunday papers. Then he turned and looked back through his peep-hole again.

Everything slept this afternoon. Outside, the countryside was deep asleep. No breath of wind disturbed anything. Inside, it was just as silent, but for an odd snore from his uncle and an occasional deep sigh from the dog sleeping at his feet. He went over to his aunt.

"Now, Aunty?"

His aunt reached across and shook her husband's sleeve.

"Harold . . . Harold, the boy's ready to go . . . Harold."

His uncle sucked a great breath, stood up, stretched and said,

"Right-ho, are we all ready to go then?" as though *he* was the one that had been waiting to go out ever since lunch.

Percy pulled on his boots and coat and went over to his aunt to have his scarf tied round his head, knotted under his chin and both ends wrapped across his chest with the windcheater zipped up so high that he could hardly swallow. All this was because of his bad chest and his aunt never let him go out without first winding him up in this great prickly thing. Percy had come to stay for two weeks to get strong again and his aunt was going to see that he went back completely better.

"If he starts his coughing he's to come back straight away, Harold."

His uncle was in the scullery and there was no answer.

As Percy followed his uncle out into the cold air, it almost did make him cough and he bit on the knot of the scarf to stifle it. Following his uncle across the yard, he heard the scullery door open behind him and the dog Galstone came racing out and the door banged too again.

His uncle was a friendly, rough sort of man who smelt of pipe smoke. He never said a great deal but grinned and nodded or winked or shrugged or would give the thumbs up where he could avoid actually speaking, and Percy liked that. All this was very different from his father, who was a much rounder, softer, neater kind of man, probably because he worked in a hospital.

"Whereabouts are they, Uncle?" His uncle nodded in the direction that they were going.

"Petersplosh Wood," he said, "if they haven't moved."

"Is it the same gypsies every year. I mean are they the same people that came last year?"

"No. Last year there were three families there," said his uncle. "This year there's only old Lias." He started counting on his fingers. "There's Lias Doyle, his wife and mother, that's three. His daughter and son-in-law and their baby, that's five and four or five little ones. We allow them to stay there every year and in exchange they clear the wood. Make a pretty good job of it too. They keep us stocked up at the house and sell what's left. It works very well really, but we don't see much of them."

His uncle fell silent again after this unusually long speech and nothing was said until Percy, hoping to get his uncle going again, asked,

"Why don't you let them stay with you all the year round, Uncle?"

His uncle just knocked his pipe out on his heel and carried on walking.

Percy was about to ask his uncle again when he said,

"Because they're travelling folk, that's why. They're travellers. It's their life, moving from one place to another." He puffed on his pipe. "It's in their blood. They could no more stay put in one place than old Galstone there could stop wagging his tail. I've felt sorry for them sometimes, but then again I've seen them early on a summer morning, six or seven caravans in a line, rumbling along the road. Women riding up on the waggons, the men leading the horses, dogs and children all strung out behind. Lord, I'm telling you, son, they looked so grand I could have gone with them, and left the whole damn lot behind!"

He stopped, took his pipe out of his mouth and looked at Percy. "No need to repeat any of all this to your aunt, is there boy?" and gave a nod.

Petersplosh Wood lay about two miles from the farm and as they went down into the valley they could see cats ice covering the puddles and in the shadow white frost still unmelted on the grass. The wood had a wide path cut through it that the hay-waggons used in the summer to come home from the fields, but at the moment it was very overgrown. Percy could see where some carts had gone through recently and there were hoof marks in the frozen mud. The temperature dropped quite noticeably in the wood and the stillness was interrupted only by a dog barking and the sound of metal being struck with a hammer. His uncle led the way, lashing at the overgrown brambles with his stick.

Lying over a hedge by the path there was some washing, quite frozen solid. Amongst it Percy noticed a pair of grey looking long-johns, so stiff they could probably have stood on their own two legs.

In a clearing just off the track, the family of travellers had made themselves at home.

Two things struck Percy at the same time. One was that it was incredible that grown-ups should actually live in a wood and secondly, that the travellers themselves and their caravans

looked so completely part of the scene that you
could have looked into that clearing and almost
not have seen them.

One of the older travellers who was lying
stretched out on the frozen ground, pulled himself to his feet at the approach of Percy and his
uncle and, pushing his hat back off his face,
stepped over the fire to greet them.

"Afternoon to you, Mr. Woodson, Sir. An' I
was only saying to the missus that we 'adn't 'ad
no sight of yourself these last two weeks or
more." He shouted at one of the small children,
"Go tell Queeny Mushti Woodson an' his young
friend is 'ere an' will be taking tea wiv us."

A little girl of about six years, wearing a thin
dress and no shoes at all, ran to the biggest of the
wooden caravans, which had a light shining
inside, and shouted something up the steps. A

space was made for them both at the fire and a box pulled up for them to sit on. His uncle and Lias Doyle were chatting like old friends, mostly about how the work in the wood was going. As they talked, Percy couldn't take his eyes off Lias or the younger traveller who sat next to him poking the fire with a stick. He noticed that their clothes were old but were not country clothes like those of his uncle. Lias wore a black suit and waistcoat, but even so, he looked anything but smart. It wasn't the sort of suit you would hang in a wardrobe every night as his father did. It had creased and worn with Lias and looked more as if it was a part of him. Their faces were brown and leathery with little dark shiny eyes in them. They both wore wide-brimmed black hats, pushed to the back of their heads.

As he looked at Lias Doyle, another thought came to him quite clearly, and that was, that these travellers in the wood, living out in all weathers the whole year round, seemed to Percy to look like some little woodland creatures. Yes, Lias Doyle reminded him of a shrew perhaps or a stoat or badger or mole; the family looked far more like a mixture of these than any people that he knew and once he began picturing them like this, he couldn't see them in any other way.

The door of the big caravan opened and Queenation, Lias's wife, came down the steps carefully carrying a tray. As she came towards them, Percy's uncle rose to his feet and Percy did the same although they were the only two to move.

"Now don't you go a-disturbin' of yourself, Mr. Woodson, I was only saying to my husband that we 'adn't seen no sign of you or your good lady."

"How are you, Mrs. Doyle?" inquired his uncle.

Queenation laid down the tray and Percy was surprised to see it set out with three beautiful white and gold cups with roses round them and a fat teapot on little legs in the same design. They looked so clean and fresh and delicate that they stood out sharply from everything else about them.

"Lovely cups, Mrs. Doyle, aren't they Uncle." Percy felt slightly foolish for a moment until he saw it had pleased Mrs. Doyle.

"I see you're a young man what's got an eye for finery and what knows a good thing when he sees it," she said to him approvingly. "Them belonged to me poor dear Gran what's long dead, bless her, an' I only got them three left thanks to the way he do drive my poor waggon and make it bump so." She jerked her finger at Lias.

Water was poured from the big black kettle   15

that had been steaming gently on its chain since their arrival and the teapot stirred with a piece of twig. It was very strong tea, made with condensed milk and very, very sweet. Besides this, it tasted woody and smoky.

It was the best tea he had ever tasted, he told his uncle on their way back to the farm, and his uncle agreed with him.

"When Mr. Doyle called out 'Kooshti Bok', what did he mean, Uncle? He said 'Kooshti Bok, young 'un,' to me when we said goodbye."

"That's Romany. Kooshti means good, I think, I've heard him use it before. They have Romany words for nearly everything. I should think 'kooshti bok' means 'good luck'".

"Kooshti," said Percy, "Kooshti." He called Galstone over. "There's a kooshti dog. What's 'dog' in Romany, Uncle?"

"That I don't know, son."

*　　*　　*

"We had kooshti tea, Aunty, in real china cups!" was the first thing Percy said when he got in.

"Did you indeed," said his aunt, unwinding him from his scarf. "You like our gypsies then."

After supper and his reading lesson, he kissed his uncle goodnight (and got his bottom pinched in return).

He kissed his aunt. "Goodnight, dear. Hop straight into bed. I'll be up in a moment."

"Kooshti Bok," he called out as he got to the door. 'I wonder what goodnight is in Romany,' he said to himself as he climbed the stairs. 'Kooshti something'. Then he had another one of his thoughts. "I could go and ask them."

The Old Lady's Story

The next day was windy and cold, and so was the day following, but the day after that, Wednesday, was brilliantly clear and sunny.

Percy had thought a great deal about the travellers in the wood. He wondered what they had done whilst it had been so windy. Perhaps they didn't mind the cold. On Sunday none of them had worn an overcoat or gloves or anything like that, and it was remembering this that made him refuse to wear his big coat today and take the scarf off as soon as he was out of sight of the house, and stuff it in his pocket.

The waggons were still there and the fire smoking quietly but there was no sign of anyone about. He stood on the edge of the clearing. He didn't want to barge in without an invitation.

19

Suddenly a dog started a furious barking and pulling on its chain. A very old woman poked her head out from one of the waggons.

"You want somethin', boy?" She came slowly down the steps of the waggon backwards. "Them others 'ave gorn orf . . . Shut yer row will yer," she shouted at the dog, and it slunk back under the waggon without another sound.

Tipping some dirty water from a bowl into the hedge, she called out, "You come over 'ere, young man. I don't 'ear so good."

Percy went over to where she had taken her seat on the bottom step.

"'e won't 'ert yer," she said, jerking her head at the dog. "You 'bide in these parts, boy?"

"I beg your pardon?" said Percy politely.

"Oo – begs my pardon, ain't that pretty," she said to herself. "You live round 'ere, son?"

"Yes, up at the farm."

"And you comes all the way over just to see us poor travellers?"

"Yes, I hope you don't mind."

The old lady looked at him. "It's company for a poor old woman what gits left alone all the day. Them childer is off in the woods. They'm meant to git me the wood for me fire but they gorn off . . . drat 'em."

"I could get wood for you," said Percy. "I'd like to."

"Yes, you could do that for a poor old woman what ain't got nobody in the world to 'elp 'er. You do that, son, but no green stuff, mind, that do make the fire smoke and affects me poor eyes dreadful."

Percy was glad to be doing something and hauled dead branches out of the wood until he had a large pile.

"Is that enough?" he asked, panting. "I can get you lots more."

The old lady nodded and started breaking off pieces and laying them over the fire. Percy did the same and watched how she made them into a wigwam shape and he did the same on his side. She bent down and, putting her head nearly into the fire, gave one long blow, straightened up and returned to her seat. Percy followed, and, looking back, saw flames already licking at the fresh wood.

"I kin see you knows about fires, boy. Who learnt you to make fires the Romany way?" Percy was going to say that he had only copied her but she asked questions in a way that made you feel they didn't really need answering.

The old lady was cutting parsnips into long thin strips using a fat handled, sharp little knife and they sat in silence for a while. Somewhere, way off in the wood, he could hear the shouting of the other children. The dog that barked at him earlier came slinking up and sniffed him all over but backed out of reach as he lifted his hand to stroke it.

"You read, boy? You read what's written down in books?"

Percy nodded.

"You so young and you kin read, and write too, I 'spect."

Percy nodded again.

"I knows things what you won't never find in

books," she said. "No, boy, not the things I know. Me mother taught me, boy, an' her mother taught her. Herbs and cures, boy, what the Romany has knowed ever since he first started his wanderings. You won't never find them written down in no fancy books."

She went on slicing the parsnips with hardly a glance at what she was doing or at Percy. A pretty little guinea fowl was pecking round her feet and there were several more by the fire, spreading their wings in the heat and kicking up ashes over themselves.

"My father's a doctor," said Percy. "He cures peoples' hearts if they stop suddenly. At his hospital they . . ."

"And a very clever gentleman I dare say he is," she interrupted. "But the Romany don't have no truck with 'em, son. Leastways, not the time when I'm talking about. It's different nowadays with them National Medicals all fer free. That son-in-law of mine is getting his electrical

23

shocks what they gives 'im for 'is back right at this minute an' I don't say that, in some ways, times ain't changed fer the good. But the Romany had his own cures, son, what he made up fer 'iself. 'E 'ad to, son. In them days we couldn't always get a doctor to come to us and then again we didn't always have the money to settle the man with.''

After a moment she went on, "Up in they big 'ospitals of yourn they is a-doin' what the Romany has done fer 'undreds of years. Fer instance, if a man's 'eart is weakly and starts a-flutterin', we crushed the flowers of fox-glove and gives 'em to 'im in a drink. I heard from a traveller what knowed, that them doctors is just a-doin' the same thing. You kin ask your own father, you ask 'im if that ain't what he puts in 'is pretty pills. And if a traveller got a pain in 'is poor 'ead we gives 'im bark from the willow tree boiled up, and ain't that just what them little aspirins is a-made from. These ain't no old woman's fancies I'm a-givin' you, son. This traveller was a-telling me that if a man cuts hisself bad and there's no a-stopping of his bleeding, up in they big 'ospitals they squirts somethin' in 'im what works like a tiny net round the wound to catch the blood. But even as tiny childer, we Romanies knowed that to bind a wound with a cob-web done the same thing.''

The old lady pointed at him with her knife.

"Nature is 'ard, son, and sometimes it seems there's no heart in her at all. But a Romany knows, son, that if she robs a man of his 'ealth with one hand she offers 'im a cure with the other. It's all 'ere son, 'ere in the 'edges. That's where a Romany knows to look."

She picked up another parsnip and stopped. "The Romany knowed these things and 'e took what 'e knowed to the 'ouse dweller what had long forgot it. But them times is passing, my son. The Romany hisself is fergettin' along with 'em."

Percy sat very still, thinking over what the old lady had said. His father often talked of his work at the hospital, or at least, he listened when his father might be telling his mother. Even though he was interested, it was very difficult to follow. But what he had just heard fascinated him. Particularly that pills and medicine were made up from plants, but more than that, plants that you could find here, in England, in this wood.

While he thought about this, the old lady had unwrapped a bundle of bacon scraps and was pulling off the rind with her fingers. Now and again she tossed a piece of rind to the dog who swallowed it without a single chew and stood with his whole attention fixed on her hands.

The dogs the other side of the clearing were

barking again and through the gap bounced a low trolley pulled by a brown pony. It hit a tree stump and stopped dead.

"Whoa there, will yer," shouted Lias unneccessarily and dropping the reins climbed laboriously down from the driving seat.

Queenation with her daughter and tiny baby and the young man Percy had seen the other day were sitting on the back. The sudden halt had sent them into a pile on top of each other and as they helped each other down, Queenation shouted something at her husband. They came across the clearing, each of the women carrying a large square basket of shopping. One of the baskets had groceries in it and the other was full of loaves. The man carried the baby on his shoulder.

"He's broke every bone in me poor body and nigh killed us besides. The man's dinillo," she shouted vexedly.

"'Allo!" she said, all sign of her crossness disappearing, "it's the pretty young man from the farm what's took a fancy to me china. 'As 'e been good company to you Ma? D'you like sweeties, son? Course 'e does. Give him a sweet, Wanda. Ain't the vittles on yet Ma? I see them childer got plenty of wood for ye, bless their li'l 'earts." All this was said with hardly a pause. She hoisted her basket up and went up the steps of her waggon and the door closed behind her.

Wanda broke off a piece of chocolate and handed it to Percy. "Go on, you 'ave it," she insisted. Another piece was given to her Gran and she pushed a piece into her husband's mouth just as he was about to lick his cigarette paper. Wanda took a piece from her own mouth and pushed it into the baby's. All of them sucked in silence. Then Wanda picked up her basket, took the baby on her hip. "Get his titty-bottle, it's on the trolley somewheres", she told the young man, and went across to her own waggon. The young man stood for a moment longer,

27

finished rolling his cigarette, stuck it in his mouth and, with a good natured nod at Percy, followed his wife across the clearing, taking a light from the fire as he passed.

Lias Doyle came across carrying the pony's harness over his shoulder and dropped it down heavily, putting both hands on his hips, he straightened his back with a grunt.

"That 'lectrical treatment do wonders for me back," he said, "but it do stiffen up so after. Still all of us 'as got our troubles, ain't we?" He took a cigarette from behind his ear. "Your uncle was a-tellin me that you is poorly in the chest."

Percy nodded. "Yes, but it's much better now though, thank you."

"What can we give our young friend for his chest, Ma?" he called out to the old lady who was going up her steps.

"I'll think on it, son," she called back.

Lias lit his cigarette with a match. "They come from all over to see her," he said. "When her 'usband was still alive they travelled in two waggons, one for themselves and the childer, the other was full of medicine and ointments and balms what they made up. They was knowed all over the south of England. Not as you'd ever guess, poor old gal, she don't never talk about it now."

Amesbury

On Saturday, Percy sat beside his uncle in the landrover. They were driving to the cattle market at Amesbury. It was a lovely run, up over the rounded grassy hills specked with sheep then down the other side through twisting lanes and through the trees and streams and villages that collect in the valleys. Up on the hills there is only sky and clouds and grass.

People come from all over the district to Amesbury, bringing livestock to sell or buy or just to look around and discuss the ups and downs of the prices. In the old days, his uncle said, cattle and sheep, pigs and geese all used to come to the market on foot and would fill the

29

streets of Amesbury while they waited to go into the auction ring. Farmers and their farm-hands came to enjoy the company after a week out on their farms and to spend the afternoon in the beer tent boasting and swapping gossip. Today it was as busy and noisy as ever as they wandered round the long rows of pens. The men at the market wore various types of country dress and it was easy to tell from what they wore whether they were wealthy farmers, or bailiffs or farm-hands.

Percy had to follow his uncle and his two farmer friends closely, if he didn't want to lose them altogether. His uncle seemed to know a lot of people there.

The place that really was packed was the beer tent and his uncle and friends were making for that now. Inside it was thick with tobacco smoke and noise and loud talking and laughing. His uncle brought him out a pork pie and a glass of ginger beer, as he wasn't allowed in and, as he nibbled his pie, he now and again caught a glimpse of his uncle at the bar. He seemed to be enjoying himself and laughed a lot.

Squeezing his way through the forest of fat back-sides and check waistcoats, he handed his uncle his empty glass.

"Can I look round on my own?" he shouted in his uncle's ear.

"Go across to the Farm Sale, boy, over the far side, and see if there's any bailing twine or barbed wire to be sold and if there is you get back here smartish. I'll be here a while yet."

"Does he want another drink?" asked one of his friends.

"When he gets back, Ted, I expect he'll have something. Off with you now, son. Barbed wire or twine."

Pushing his way out into the sunlight, he made his way over to the far side of the market where groups of people were picking over little piles of junk. Farm sort of junk, bundles of rakes and hoes, boxes of tools and milking equipment. Pumps, paraffin lamps, bundles of fencing posts, tractor wheels, mole traps, chicken coops and so on. It was very useful being small, you could worm your way in and out of the groups quickly. Something that he did rather fancy for himself was a bundle of rabbit skins. Now, if he could get those, he could make himself a rabbit skin suit! He found two reels of barbed wire with a bucket of rusty staples but nowhere could he see any twine. He was about to go back and report when he saw a familiar figure foraging in a box of old spanners. Percy went up to him.

"Hallo, Mr. Doyle."

"'Allo, son. You here on your own sweet lonesome?"

"No. Uncle Harry's in the beer tent."

"Good fer 'im," said Lias.

"I've got to look for some barbed wire or twine for him."

"I just seed some o' that." Lias scratched his head with the spanner he was holding. "Where the devil did I see that?"

"I know where it is Mr. Doyle, thanks. Lot forty-four."

Lias tossed the spanner back in the box and they turned to go.

"If'n you wants to see some travellers, son, you kin come over to 'The Fox', that's the pub the travellers use. If'n your uncle says it's O.K. you kin come and play with the other childer in the yard there. Then you kin ride on home along with us but only if your uncle gives 'is word on it, mind."

*   *   *

There's some wire and staples in Lot forty-four, Uncle," he shouted in his uncle's ear. Their faces seemed pinker than ever. "And Uncle, Mr. Doyle says I can go and play with his children over at the 'Fox', if you say I can. Can I, Uncle? If I keep myself wrapped up?" He zipped his windcheater up to his chin to show that he meant it. "They said I could drive home with them after."

His uncle looked thoughtful.

"Will he be having a drink now?" said his uncle's friend. "I think he's earned it."

"Mr. Doyle says it's a real travellers' pub," said Percy.

His uncle was still looking at him thoughtfully as he took a sip of beer. "I don't see the harm in it," he said simply. "Ted here's offering you another lemonade."

"No, I'll go now, Mr. Doyle told me where it is. Thank you for the drink all the same . . . sir." (he nearly said Ted.) "See you at home, Uncle."

"Choosy who he drinks with, is he?" said Ted and the three men laughed.

Percy was already half out of the tent, on his way to the real travellers' pub.

*   *   *

He crossed the spacious town square which, typical of Saturday, was full of market stalls and housewives with their big baskets. In the far corner of the square was a pub called 'The Fox and Grapes' and in the middle of this pub an archway lead to a cobbled stone yard behind. It was in this yard that the travellers were. Along the road outside were trucks and vans that Percy could tell were travellers' waggons. They had a sort of look about them which he was beginning to recognise. A rather battered look, and hand-painted in light blue or maroon.

In the yard itself he saw the Doyle's trolley with its shafts in the air and children playing all over it. Their pony, with its harness still on, was munching quietly at a tub of geraniums. There was one other horse too, tied to a drainpipe, which was giving little snorts and showing its teeth. On the sunny side of the yard, he could see Mrs. Doyle's mother chattering away to another old couple and Percy could see that when they laughed, which they did often, they hadn't got a single tooth between them.

Travellers were making their way up and down the steps, treading over the people sitting there, to the saloon bar and, through this door, 35

he could hear someone playing an accordian and a voice singing with it. There was a thunderous burst of applause as it finished and much stamping and shouting. It was a very cheerful scene.

Queenation leaned out of the window and handed out bottles of lemonade and packets of crisps to her clamouring children beneath, like a mother thrush. Seeing Percy standing in the sunlight, she shouted something over her shoulder and Lias Doyle's flushed face appeared above that of his wife.

"Hold on, young 'un," he called and drew back out of sight. A minute or two later, he appeared on the steps with a bottle of beer in his hand.

"Cop a-hold of that young 'un." He waved the bottle at Percy.

They were giving him beer, real beer! He was delighted. Lias must have read the expression on his face because he said, "That's shandy, son, got lemonade in it. Put hairs on yer chest like ship's cables. Kooshti Bok," and he raised his own glass and drank.

"Kooshti Bok to you, Mr. Doyle" said Percy and took a swig. It stung in his nose but it was lovely and he took another. What a day this was. Drinking almost real beer with his traveller friends in a travellers' pub. He just wished his brother could see him now.

A traveller, much heavier than Lias, came over to them. "We going to have this little deal then, Lias my son?" The man went over to Lias's brown pony.

"He wants to swap his black horse over there for my little mare," Lias said out of the corner of his mouth, "but he wants twenty-five pounds on top of it and I ain't keen to part with it."

He went and joined the man and, the other Travellers, sensing a deal in the air, brought their drinks over. The two men went over to the black horse.

"I tell 'e Cutter, I don't rightly like the looks of 'im," said Lias in a whiney voice, "'e looks frisky to me."

"Frisky!" Cutter said scornfully. Frisky. I tell you, Lias Doyle, and it's as true as what I'm standing 'ere, that's the quietest 'orse what I ever 'ad. Ain't that right Ma?" He turned to the toothless one on the seat behind him.

"'E'm quiet as a baby, 'e'm as gentle as a lamb," she said loyally, and went back to her conversation with hardly a pause.

"Go on, 'ave a deal wiv 'im, Lias," one or two of the onlookers shouted encouragement.

"I tell you what I've a mind to do, Cutter," said Lias, "we'll have a straight chop."

"A straight . . . !" Cutter pretended to be lost for words and the unfairness of the suggestion had taken his breath away. "Put twenty-five pound notes in me 'and and we've got ourselves a deal."

"A straight chop," Lias insisted and it was his turn to praise the sturdiness and strength of his little pony. "I'll give you ten one pound notes what I got here in me pocket," said Lias extending his hand.

"Go on, take the man's money," came voices from the onlookers.

"Give us yer money then, and may I never see my wife and little ones again." Cutter held out his hand but instead of shaking as Percy had expected, they slapped each other's open palm. That settled the deal and the others drifted back to their seats on the steps and Lias and Cutter disappeared inside the Saloon.

Percy played with the other children on the trolley, it was quite a simple game, just pulling each other off and scrambling back up again. Singing had started and a mouth-organ was playing something very slow and sad. Then everybody came down the steps, filling the yard; some of the men were staggering slightly and the women began sorting out the children.

When the families had settled in their carts and lorries, the men climbed wearily in and one by one the old lorries pulled away with their shouted goodbyes.

The Doyles were the last to leave as Lias was having a lot of trouble with the fiddly straps and buckles of the harness as he altered it to fit the new horse. Finally, it was ready and Lias led them out of the yard and into the busy traffic. He walked nearly out of town before sitting up on the footboard and taking the reins.

"Garn . . . Away with yer. Let's see what yer made of," he shouted.

The horse trotted along easily with his load of Doyles.

"See how pretty he picks his feet, Ma," he called over his shoulder. "We've had a good chop 'ere!"

They were making good speed and there was

hardly a sound from the trolley on its rubber wheels, just the clop-clop of the horses heels and the rhythmic jingle of the harness. Mrs. Doyle was half asleep and so were the two youngest children against her legs. Percy and Wingate (the only other child old enough to drink shandy) sat perched on the back with their legs dangling over the edge, watching the road slip away beneath them. It was a lovely way to travel, surrounded by the open air like this and to be able to see the banks so closely and the trees high above your head like clouds.

The new horse kept giving its little snorts but it was pleased to be moving again after its tiresome day tied up in the 'Fox and Grapes' yard.

Through the village of Wimbourn, just this side of Splitwillow Bridge, work was going on widening part of the road. Workmen using picks and shovels followed behind a man using a pneumatic drill and it was the noise of this drill that caused the new horse to prick up its ears. The nearer they got to the dreadful racket the more the horse began to veer from side to side of the road and Lias was having a difficult time to control it, his shouting completely drowned in the machine-gun noise of the drill. Percy wondered why the workman didn't have enough sense to switch it off until they passed but, one

look at the stupid grin on the man's face, and he saw that the man knew perfectly well the trouble he was causing.

By now the horse was really frightened and went forward in a crabwise fashion until suddenly, rearing right up on its back legs, it lunged forward and took off at a gallop, hooves flying and ears back!

Lias hauled on the reins, "Hold on, everybody, hold on!" he yelled. "Whoa! damn you! Easy there, Easy!"

Percy gripped the sides of the trolley with all his strength as the hedges flew by him.

The horse with its head pulled so far back lost its sight of the road and went up over the soft curb, down a shallow bank and floundered into a muddy stream; halting suddenly at the shock of cold water. A strangled shout followed by a great 'splash' echoed round the river banks as Lias

Doyle pitched head first into the stream and thrashed about on his back in the shallow water, swearing furiously.

"He's drowned us!" howled Queenation, who had scooped her children into her two arms, "he's drowned us all . . . the loony!"

Actually, it was only the front two wheels that were under the water, the back wheels were still on the stony ground at the river's edge. Lias hauled himself over to the footboard and was hanging there coughing and swearing in turns. Exactly what it was that Lias called his horse I don't feel that I ought to repeat here, but in any case, for all the difference it made he might just as well have bellowed at the moon. His horse was placidly helping himself to a long, refreshing drink.

Percy and Wingate had been thrown on top of each other when the cart came to its abrupt stop and were sorting themselves out; and now, apart from the children sobbing quietly and Lias's cough, everything was suddenly extremely peaceful.

A man's voice called out from above them.

"You all right down there, Doyle?"

Percy saw his uncle silhouetted at the top of the bank peering anxiously down. Lias, unable to speak raised his hand weakly. Percy's uncle waded out up to his knees and, collecting the little ones in his arms set them down on the soft grass. Percy remembered his unfinished pie in his pocket and broke the poor squashed thing into three pieces which the little ones chewed on happily. Queenation took uncle's hand and daintily lifting her heavy skirt jumped down very gracefully for such a large lady.

Everyone seemed to be feeling much better except, perhaps, poor Lias who was up to his waist in the freezing water undoing the sopping harness. The horse was freed and led to the side where it shook itself like a dog and moved off to graze along the river bank.

The landrover was brought down and the little cart towed with a chain backwards up the bank and onto the road. Percy liked the way the two men worked without fuss and Lias's refusal to take the slightest notice of his being thoroughly soaked.

"A drop o' water wouldn't kill 'im," was all he said.

Queenation rolled him a cigarette from the black tobacco she kept in a tin under her skirt and lit it for him which started the poor man on another furious bout of coughing.

Percy's uncle insisted on driving Mrs. Doyle to the top of their lane.

"You chavies go get the fire goin' so's that foolish father o' yourn can dry hisself when he gits 'ome," she told the children.

Lias was left to harness his steaming horse and follow them back, refusing to take any more help from anybody.

"It wasn't Mr. Doyle's fault, that workman wouldn't switch off his machine and the horse bolted," said Percy indignantly, as they drove home over the fields. "They did it on purpose."

"Not everyone's as fond of the gypsies as you are, you know," said his uncle, and would only shrug his shoulders at Percy's genuinely puzzled question, "But, why, Uncle?"

* * *

Percy's aunt wanted to know how he had got so muddy and what on earth had they been doing at the market to get so wet? Percy told her the story of the Doyle's new horse and its short cut into the stream but somehow in the telling of it it didn't come out that he had been riding with them at the time.

That night Percy lay in his bed thinking over the incredible swear words Mr. Doyle had used on his new horse and repeated them over and over to himself.

"I wonder what they mean," he said. Closing his eyes he went over the whole scene again in his mind.

"I don't think I'll ask him," he murmured, "not this time."

The Captain's Story

"Will I be here for Christmas, Uncle?" asked
Percy, two days after the incident in the river.

"I don't know, boy. I thought you'd be going
home. Why? Would you like to stay?"

"Yes please, Uncle."

He said 'yes please' but he would also like to
go home for Christmas but, then again, he would
like to spend it with his uncle and aunt as well.

"I don't mind, Uncle. Whatever you say," he
added.

"Well, you talk to your Mum when I ring her   47

tonight. See what she says. O.K.?"

"I would like to stay," said Percy finally, "if I can." He had just realised that they could send his presents to him at the farm.

"Good," said his uncle, and winked.

*   *   *

"Is it all right if I go to see Mr. Doyle this afternoon?" he asked his aunt whilst he dried up the lunch things, "Just to see if he's all right."

"What do you always want to go down to the gypsies for?" said his aunt. "Wouldn't you like to play with Janette?" Janette was a girl who lived in a cottage further up the lane.

"Yes, but she doesn't get out of school 'til late and then it's dark and we have to play at her house."

"Well, what's wrong with that?" said his aunt reasonably.

"No . . . nothing," said Percy.

But he did ask her again later and this time wasn't so easily talked out of it; but he was definitely to be back in time for tea.

He ran across the fields. The travellers always made him welcome and he felt no shyness about going there.

All the Doyles were working round a blazing fire when he got there, even Wingate. They were sitting surrounded by piles of holly and laurel branches. Wanda and Dicklo were using moss that the little ones had collected and binding it onto circular wire frames. These frames looked like the wire part of a dart-board and were about the same size. They were passed on to Lias and Queenation and her old mother who were skilfully binding in the sprays of holly. Percy recognised them as Christmas wreaths that people hang on their front doors. None of them wore any protection to their hands and they all of them worked very swiftly. As soon as they finished making one another was started.

"Go git the kettle and fill it from the churn, son," Lias told Percy as soon as he arrived. When the kettle was boiling, Mrs. Doyle got up and, after brushing off the prickly leaves that stuck to her apron, brought over the basket with all the tea things in and set them out. Lias straightened his back with a grunt.

"Wreaths, son, what we makes up every year for the market up Lunnon."

Tin mugs of tea were handed round and it pleased Percy that he had been included automatically. He cupped his hands round the mug and sipped the hot, sweet tea.

"'E can 'elp Wingate cut the 'olly," said Mrs. Doyle.

"Would you like to make up one of your own,

son?" asked Lias. "There's something they won't learn you at no school."

"You sit alongside Wanda, she'll show you 'ow it's done," said Mrs. Doyle. "When she's 'ad 'er tea."

A lorry was heard grinding its way down the lane and into the clearing bounced an old, dark blue truck. A big man, a traveller, came over to the fire. He nodded to everyone there.

"'Ows you keeping then, Captain?" asked Lias. Captain took a cup from Mrs. Doyle and he, Lias and Dicklo went over to his lorry and started to load it with the finished wreaths.

"The res'll be ready Sat'day," called Lias as the old lorry drove off. They could hear him grinding his gears all the way up the lane. Tea dregs were flicked hissing into the fire and the cups put back in the basket. Work started again. Wanda showed Percy how to bind in the moss with the thin, soft wire and he slowly and carefully copied her.

They worked on in silence.

"Why do you call him 'Captain', Wanda?" asked Percy. "Is he a sailor?"

"No, I don't fink so," she replied. "He weren't a sailor, was he, Pa?"

"No, he i'n't no sailor," said Lias. "Mind you 'es done a bit of sailin' in 'is time." He was chuckling. "'Ain't 'e, Ma?"

Mrs. Doyle laughed.

"There's a bit of a story, see," said Lias, "as to how he got his name." He blew his nose on his handkerchief. And he told them the story of how he came to be called 'The Captain'.

*   *   *

This is the story Lias told:-

A group of travellers were camped by a bend in the River Findrim, just above Wrexford. The raspberry and strawberry picking were over, and, as there had been a dry summer, there was a week's delay before they could start earning good money from picking up potatoes. They welcomed the chance to relax and 'The Carpenters' Arms' at Wrexford was enjoying an unexpected boom in custom, especially at mid-day. When they opened their doors in the morning, the travellers would be waiting to go in and would only leave when the doors were closed in the afternoon. The travellers would then come reeling home to their waggons to sleep off the effects; waking later, refreshed and looking forward to the evening's drinking. So, in this way, the week passed very pleasantly. On the last morning of their holiday, the drinking had been heavier than ever and, of the little group of men that left 'The Carpenters' Arms' only half of them managed to arrive home. Gelsnip was one

of these. He made his way along the line of
wooden caravans until he recognised the familiar
carving of his own waggon and, after several
unsuccessful attempts finally got himself to the
top of the steps and into the waggon, where he
stood, triumphant but unsteady. He bent down
and groped for his feet but in his present state of
wooziness he was in no mood to fiddle about with
laces and raising his foot he tugged off his boot.
On his two legs he had been unsteady, but on

one he had no chance at all. He reeled backwards and landed seat first on the little coal burning stove that is just inside the door of every travellers' waggon. This had been made up by his wife before she left to go shopping in Wrexford, and was burning steadily. He sat there reflecting quietly for a moment whilst frantic messages went from his backside up to his brain that it was hot and getting hotter. When the message did get through, he jumped up with a shout. He groped his way down the inside of his waggon to his bed and hauled himself over the edge. He was asleep as his head hit the pillow, and snoring.

Outside, the encampment was bathed in the sunshine of a glorious summer's afternoon. Whoops and shouts of laughter from the other travellers came up through the open window. A fly droned against the tiny lantern windows in the ceiling of Gelsnip's caravan, itself half drunk with the heat.

One of Gelsnip's boots was still on his foot. The other was roasting gently on top of the range where Gelsnip had left it. A thin file of blue smoke began to fill the waggon which thickened with every moment and before long it had found an escape through the open window.

"Fire!" shouted a voice outside. "Waggon's a-fire!"

"Water," shouted another. "Git some water!"

"Water! Quick! The man's waggon is a-burning!"

Fire, more than any other element, is the travellers' great fear. Their wooden waggons once alight, go up like tinder, and, as they only ever carry enough water for their immediate needs, there is rarely enough to be able to save them.

A bucket of water came sloshing through the window and left everything in the middle of the waggon dripping.

"Get her down to the river."

"Where's Gelsnip?" somebody shouted. "Where's Gelsnip, tell 'im 'is waggons a-fire!"

"Get her down to the river!" insisted the voice, "Put her out down there."

The reality of the situation was working the mens' minds clearer, as thick rolls of smoke poured out of the window.

"Take the shafts!" Three men lifted a shaft under their arms and two more took the other.

"Together now, one . . . two . . . three . . . HEAVE! . . . And again . . . HE-AVE . . . HEAVE!"

The waggon which was fortunately near the river and facing it, lumbered slowly over the grass and tipped slightly, ready for its journey down the long shallow bank to the water.

"PUSH!" shouted a drunken voice from the back commanding some newly arrived help.

"STEADY!" shouted the men on the shafts.

"Hold hard!" came alarmed voices from the front, "Whoa! Steady on will yer."

"'Old 'er, 'old 'er!" came back the voices from the front, now edged with real panic.

"'She's a-going!" screamed one. "JUMP!"

The five men on the shafts who had been digging their heels into the soft ground leapt in all directions to avoid being squashed under the iron-shod wheels as the waggon trundled steadily towards the river.

It was going at a good speed by the time it hit the water and continued a third of the way out into the wide, shallow river before coming to a halt in a sea of bubbles. The wheels were completely covered by the water but it floated neatly underneath the floor of the waggon with hardly a ripple.

The horrified onlookers lay where they had fallen and watched the retreating waggon with round, helpless eyes. They were quite, quite sober now.

"Gawd!" said one, speaking for them all, "Oh Gawd, . . . He'll kill us!"

Gelsnip's painted waggon stood in the river where it had rolled. Smoke still came from the window but much less now and more came cheerfully from the little chimney. Gelsnip's Caravan looked for all the world as though a colourful river boat had dropped anchor in the bend of a peaceful river on a lovely summer's afternoon.

Whether a message got through to Gelsnip's brain via his nostrils picking up the acrid smell of burning leather or, whether it was through his ears, tuning in to the unusual sound of water lapping underneath the waggon, I don't know. Possibly these two messengers had combined in a single determined assault on his sleeping fortress of a brain and had managed to make their report. Anyway, the result was that he awoke. That is, one eyelid slid open and a watery, pale blue eye motionlessly took in the scene before it. Then the other eye swiftly opened to confirm the findings of the first. What his eyes reported back was, that, outside of the pretty cut glass windows of the front door was – a great deal of water.

Gelsnip swung himself heavily out of bed and gazed first out of the right window and then through the left. Outside of both was – water. He pushed open the cut glass windows of the front door and stared blankly at the water that stretched to the bank opposite. Gelsnip opened the lower section of the door and stepped out onto the footboard as he had done a thousand

times before. There, below his feet and gently lapping against the edge was – water.

A rowing boat appeared suddenly in front of him. A young man was pulling at the oars and a pretty girl sat opposite trailing her fingers over the side.

"'Afternoon," called the young man. The girl gave him a wave and a smile and they passed on down river.

"Oi!" Gelsnip started to call after them but they were too far away. He stood swaying in the doorway then reached under his arm for a bottle of beer he had in his pocket. Opening it on his teeth, he took a long swig and turned back inside the waggon. He peered through the side windows again; it was water all right. Sitting on his bed, he drained the last of his beer and lay back on the pillows. He watched the dance of reflected lights on the ceiling until its hypnotising effect slid his eyelids closed again.

"Water," he murmured.

The camp, meanwhile, had become a hive of activity. One of the boys had stripped and was swimming out with a rope tied to his waist which he bound round the back axle of the waggon, just below the surface. Two horses were brought down to the water's edge and the job of hauling the caravan back was begun. It lumbered quietly out of the water, up the bank and back onto its old resting place, dripping quietly. They congratulated each other.

"When 'e comes back we won't none of us say nothing."

"What 'e don't know won't 'ert 'im," was generally agreed as the best attitude to take to the affair.

About tea time, Mrs. Kelsey arrived back at her waggon and Gelsnip woke to find his wife poking him in the stomach shouting, "Look what you done to my stove! 'Ow'm I a-going to get that orf? That's the only pair what you've got. Serves you right, you drunken-headed old fool. What you keep a-looking out of the window for?"

Gelsnip pushed past his wife and hobbled down the steps of his waggon. He looked round the camp. The waggons were there, his friends were there sitting round the fire minding their own business. Everything looked just as it always did.

He rolled himself a cigarette and as he turned to go back up the steps his eye was attracted to something. When he saw what it was, he straightened up quickly and then bent forward to inspect it again. Caught round a bolt on one of the shafts was a small piece of water weed. He took it in his hand and went thoughtfully back inside.

That evening, as always, the travellers adjourned to 'The Carpenters' Arms' and as Gelsnip went in he saw something that immediately rang a bell inside his head. A young man was sitting opposite a pretty girl at a table in the far corner. Seeing him, they both smiled, and the girl called over,

"Evening Captain. Still moored up at the Creek?"

"It was water!" Gelsnip exploded. He looked round dangerously at the other travellers who had, every one of them, taken a step back. He stood there, his shoulders hunched, his fists clenched, studying the faces that in turn were studying his. The silence was broken by a traveller clearing his throat.

"What will you be 'aving to drink, then — Gelsnip?"

"Yeah," said another. "'Ave a drink with us . . . Captain."

* * *

" . . . And 'Captain' 'ees been ever since," said Lias, tossing the wreath he had just finished onto the pile. "'Ow about another drop of tea, Ma?" He put his fist into the small of his back and rubbed hard.

60 "Let's 'ave a look, son," he said, inspecting

Percy's wobbly looking wreath. "Not bad, son," he said kindly. "Not bad for a Gorgio."

"I'm going to give it to my mother," said Percy, "for Christmas."

"'Ain't that nice," said Mrs. Doyle loudly. "Did you 'ear that, Wingate? 'Es a-goin' to give 'is dear good mother a nice present for Christmas."

* * *

The downstairs lights of the house were on as Percy ran through the farmyard.

"Sorry I'm late, Aunty," he said kicking off his boots.

"Percy, I told you quite definitely you were to be home by . . ."

"I know, Aunty. I've been making this." He produced his wreath. Unfortunately, a sprig of holly had dropped off somewhere.

"It's very nice I'm sure, but I've been sitting here wor . . ."

"It's for you," said Percy quickly. He gave it to his aunt and plunged into all the details of how it was made.

"I thought it would look lovely hanging on your front door," he finished.

His aunt looked at Percy and then at the   61

wreath in her hands, then plonked it on his head like a bowler hat.

"All right, all right, you little Brutus," she said. "If you think it'll look so fine you'd better go and hang it there yourself."

And this he gladly did.

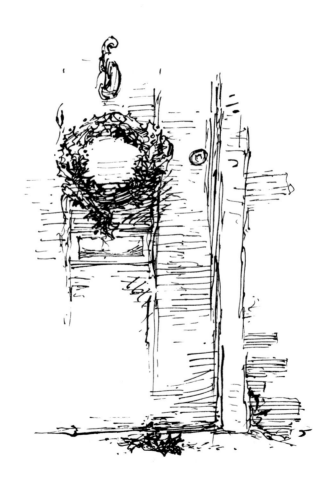

An Afternoon with Dicklo

"Where's Wanda today?" asked Percy, coming up behind Dicklo who was crouched over a fire.

"She an' Ma's gone tattin'," he said over his shoulder. Percy had found him alone at the camp heating up a piece of metal in a fire that he was making red hot with a pair of bellows.

"Tatting?" said Percy.

"Yea, hawking, selling," said Dicklo. "You come and stand here, boy, and keep this fire hot." He gave Percy the bellows and stood behind him. Putting his hands over Percy's on the handles he showed him how to work them.

63

"See? Short an' quick an' when it gets white hot in there, keep it going with long slow uns."

Whilst Percy was carefully doing this, Dicklo pulled a small piece of red hot metal out of the fire with a pair of tongs and took it over to his anvil where he gave it a great clout with his hammer, still holding the end of it in his tongs. He examined it and sparks flew as he gave it several more well aimed blows. His ingenious anvil was a lump of steel from a tractor nailed to the top of a tree stump. Dicklo pushed the metal back into the fire again and Percy worked the bellows as he had been shown, making them sound like a steam engine pulling out of the station.

"Well done, son. Keep it goin'." Dicklo crouched beside him. "Me waggons a-bustin' all over. Got to mend it up afore I chop it in the Spring."

"Chop it, you're going to chop it up?" said Percy amazed. Dicklo's wasn't a handsome, carved waggon like Mrs. Doyle's. It had metal sides and rubber tyred wheels, but even so it seemed terrible to just chop it up.

"No. Swap it, exchange it," said Dicklo. "Me an' Wanda's gettin' a lorry and trailer. I know someone what'll take me lot here and two hundred and fifty pounds what I got saved up in the Post Office besides. An' for that we'll get ourselves a right smart little outfit."

"Will you be getting rid of your horse too?" asked Percy, whose arms were really aching.

"Yep, all goin'." Dicklo pushed the wood further into the fire with his foot. "When I gets me new trailer, I'm goin' to park her in one of them Council enclosures where a man can settle an' not keep gettin' hisself moved on all the blinkin' time. When me little girl's older she kin go to school, like you. Me and me uncle's goin' to start a nice little scrap business over Slough way." He pushed his cap over his eyes and scratched the back of his head. "I 'spect I'll have another grai one day, for me little girl, like."

Percy was saying over and over in his head. 'Tatting' is 'selling', 'grai' is 'horse'; two more words for his Romany-English dictionary he was building up. He had eighteen words so far, (including these two, if he could remember them), and had worked out the meaning of nearly all of them himself without having to ask the Doyles.

"Won't you be travelling with Mr. and Mrs. Doyle then, if you go in a lorry?"

"Nope, all finished," Dicklo said, hammering furiously. "My folks has 'ad trailers for years. Wanda's Dad won't change now. He won't learn to drive a lorry. He ain't learned to drive an 'orse yet, come to that. He could get a good price for that old waggon of his. I told him them antiquey blokes is a-fallin' over theirselves to get 'em, I told 'im, but no, he won't sell, not 'im, and Queenie won't neither. Twenty or thirty years ago he'd been lucky to get a fiver for it. I've knowed folks what's had to leave their waggon alongside the verge 'cos nobody didn't want 'em. It was different then, mind you, before I was born, before the motey car come, like. A man could buy hisself a brand new waggon all carved and lined out beautiful but no one don't do that kind of work any more.'' He took a stick and poked it in the fire. The leaping flame singed his long eyelashes as he pulled it out and lit the cigarette he had been rolling. When he was puffing happily, he went on: ''Sometimes they might have to git a new waggon made up on account of the way that if a travelling man dies they sets his waggon a-fire along with all his trappin's.''

''You mean they burnt them?'' said Percy.

''Yea. Keep them bellows goin', son. Yus, burnt 'em, I 'spose you wouldn't know that. If a travellin' man's vardo ain't yagged, his spirit's still attached. It ain't free to go off, like.''

''Go off where?'' said Percy. He was preoccupied with scratching 'yag' and 'vardo' in the ashes with a twig whilst he could still remember

66

them. He guessed that they must mean 'fire' and 'waggon'.

"Just off, I 'spose," said Dicklo. "Wherever a travellin' man's spirit goes when he snuffs it. I dunno exactly where that is, like."

Dicklo took his metal out of the fire, blew on it then pushed it back again. "They tell of a Romany what was married to a house dweller an' when this Romany dies she wouldn't let them burn his waggon. Said it was a waste and that she wouldn't have nowheres to live. The man's family said if she didn't, 'is spirit would take his revenge on 'er, but she wouldn't take no heed of them and when they was walking back from the church after they'd a-buried 'im, a dreadful storm blew up. The waggon was struck by lightnin' and when the got there it was all burnt out. See, the Romany, he knows these things."

Dicklo whipped the metal out of the fire and this time took it over to his anvil where he gave it another beating. Percy came over to the tree stump.

"Do you think travellers' spirits and ordinary peoples' spirits go to the same place?" Percy shouted above the din.

"I don't know about that, brother, maybe they do, maybe they don't." Dicklo held up his work and studied it through one eye; then he turned to Percy and said,

"Tell you the truth, boy, I 'opes not. I've had enough of being pushed around by them policemens in this 'ere life to want to go a-rubbin' shoulders with them up there, being kept a-movin' round heaven all day." He went on, "Me Gran told me it was a Romany what made the nails what was used to a-crucify Jesus, though he didn't know that's what they was goin' to be used for when he made 'em, like. And them nails kept appearing to 'im, all a-glowin', ghost-like, and a-following 'im wherever he went. That's how the Romany first started his wanderin's, me Gran said, to escape from them nails. You can leave the fire be, boy. I've nearly done."

Percy watched Dicklo's face as he concentrated on his work. As he looked he could picture

69

the first gypsy, hammering out those nails at his anvil, and starting the Romany tribe off on wanderings that took them right across Europe and Asia, and, two thousand years later, here was one of the last of the Romanies, hammering at his anvil, almost his final act before giving up the travelling life for ever. It seemed as if the Romany had come a full circle.

Percy was brought back from these thoughts by a spitting, hissing from the red hot piece of metal as Dicklo plunged it into a rusty tin of water.

"Well, that's finished then," he said, collecting up his tools. "We done a good job there, you an' me. How do you fancy being a partner in me scrap metal business?" Dicklo felt behind his ear for a cigarette end. "I think right now a drop o' tea's called for, don't you? Pity to waste a good fire."

Christmas

"Your mother and father are coming to spend Christmas here at the farm, and Roy, and you'll all be going back on Boxing Day to see Gran and Granpa," Percy's aunt informed him. "I spoke to your mother on the 'phone last night, after you'd gone to bed."

"Are they taking me back with them?" Percy asked.

"Yes, dear," replied his aunt.

"Back home?" he asked.

"Yes," replied his aunt patiently.

"Oh!" said Percy, disappointment written all over his face, and he turned back to his comic.

He had forgotten 'home'. He had been away so long. Two months in hospital and two more weeks here at the farm. He had forgotten home and his brother and his room and school and friends. He had forgotten his fish, and Saturday morning cinema, and the Badgettes next door and their dog Kim. He'd forgotten his new Cub uniform and television, and his bike and its three tone hooter, and his cactus plants in the greenhouse, and his mother's home-made sweets and his rope ladder and, as he thought over all the things that he'd forgotten he suddenly, more than anything, wanted to go home.

*　　*　　*

On Thursday, Percy waited at the ticket barrier with his aunt and uncle.

"There they are! They're here!" he called back from his position at the grilled gate. "I can see them!"

People poured through the gate and his mother came through and hugged him in a great waft of perfume, his father tousled his hair and his brother Roy punched him on the arm. People were piling up behind them and they had to collect up the cases and parcels and take them out to the Landrover.

"Just look at the colour in his cheeks," exclaimed his mother. "Alice, you've done wonders with him."

"That's plenty of fresh air," said his uncle. "and good food, of course," he added.

"I like your hair, Roy," said Percy to his

brother. Roy was nearly fifteen and his hair was almost down to his shoulders. His uncle was enthusiastically shaking Roy by the hand.

"My God, he's growing, Alice. Shooting up like a hollyhock and as pretty as one too."

They stopped at the 'White Hart' on the way home and took their drinks onto the benches outside in the warm winter sun. Percy couldn't have been happier to see them all again. When he saw his aunt and mother sitting together he could see quite clearly that they were sisters. His aunt Alice was the older of the two. It seemed strange that two women so similar could have chosen such widely different men for their husbands.

As they sat in the sun, a horse, with plumes of steam coming from his nostrils, pulling a trolley, appeared jogging along the road loaded with logs and children, and, as it passed, Lias Doyle stood up and touched his cap with his whip.

"Mornin', Mr. Woodson, sir. Fine mornin'. Mornin' to you, Mrs. Woodson."

Percy's uncle saluted back with his beer glass.

"Hallo, Mr. Doyle," shouted Percy.

"Mornin', son," Lias called back and gave Percy a thumbs up. "Get over, yer poxin' blighter!" he shouted at his horse who had taken the trolley up the curb with a bump that had thrown Lias back in his seat.

"Whoever was that?" asked Percy's mother when the trolley had gone. "He seemed to know you very well, Percy."

"That's Mr. Doyle. He's a friend of mine," said Percy proudly. "I've been to tea with him lots of times, havn't I, Uncle? I've had a ride on that trolley too, we pulled him out of the river and . . ." Percy got a strong feeling that it wasn't wise to go on. He had only wanted to show his family what interesting friends he had made.

"The boy's got very attached to some gypsies that live in our wood," explained his uncle. "They're all right. I've known them on and off for over ten years."

"Well, he looked as though he hadn't had a good wash for over ten years either," said his mother coldly.

"He does wash!" said Percy indignantly. "Well, he doesn't wash much because they use all their water for tea. Mrs. Doyle's always washing clothes and things and the little ones play in the mud all the time and then they get . . . muddy," he finished lamely.

"Never mind that now," interrupted his father. "Anybody for another drink before they close?"

*   *   *

On the following morning, Percy's uncle drove them into Amesbury to do some Christmas shopping and the rest of the day was spent decorating the big kitchen with holly and ivy. It was beginning to feel really Christmasy and Percy had seen parcels brought back from Amesbury that were taken straight up to his aunt's bedroom.

Christmas Eve was lovely. A great log fire blazed away in the sitting room and they all played Scrabble, but the game had to be abandoned because of a violent argument about Percy's use of Romany words, which Roy found unacceptable. Then they sat round the fire and ate hot mince pies until they were warm and full and sleepy.

Christmas day itself was cold and grey but nobody minded, it was so warm and cheerful in the house. After the great Christmas dinner and the 'handing out presents' ceremony, everybody sprawled sleepily in front of the fire and it wasn't until then that Percy remembered something very important.

"When are we going back, Dad?" he asked.

"Tomorrow, first thing," said his father sleepily.

"But when am I going to give the Doyles their presents, then?" he asked, looking round.

There was a quietness amongst the grown ups.

His aunt said,

"Harry can take them down for you in the morning, couldn't you, Harry?"

"Oh no," said Percy. "Couldn't I take them down now, Aunt Alice?"

"You'll have to ask your father about that," replied his aunt. "It's quite a long way."

"Roy could go with you . . . Now don't look like that Roy," said his father, as Roy was making strong signs that he didn't want to go. He was lying on his back using Galstone as a pillow and had just started reading one of his Christmas books.

"I'll take the boy," said his uncle, and collected Percy's coat from the cupboard.

"All right, I'll come," said Roy, closing his book.

In the end they all went, except Percy's aunt who excused herself by saying that she had to get tea ready.

"Tea!" exclaimed uncle. "Good Lord, woman, we've only just finished lunch!" Nevertheless his aunt wouldn't come.

There was not a soul to be seen at the camp, although all three waggons had lights from their windows and a bright fire crackled away.

Percy's uncle knocked on Mrs. Doyle's door and came back down the steps, as he reached the bottom Lias's head appeared at the little cut glass windows.

"Merry Christmas to you, Doyle. We've come to pay our respects," said uncle, "and to give you this." He handed up a bottle wrapped in white tissue paper.

"That's exceedingly kind of you Gov'nor. Look at this, Queenie, Mooshti Woodson's done brought us a handsome bottle o' brandy to keep the cold from our old bones." He came down the steps.

"Come to the fire, lady, and warm yerself," Lias indicated to Percy's mother to follow him.

"You'll take some tea with us?" he asked, pulling up an oil drum for the mother to sit on, carefully wiping the top with his sleeve.

"Er . . ." said his mother. "Er . . . well . . ."

"Thank you," said his father. "We would like that very much." "My son has told us a great deal about you all. I think he has something he wants to give you."

Percy looked in his paper bag for Mr. Doyle's present, a packet of cigarette papers in Christmas wrapping.

Queenation called out from her waggon something that none of them could understand, not even Percy.

"Me missus says for you to go and join her in her waggon, M'am," said Lias to Percy's mother. "Out the draught."

He led her to the waggon, giving his hand to   79

her as she climbed the steps and disappeared inside.

Lias felt more at ease amongst the menfolk and pulled up seats for them all, kicking the fire into a blaze. Dicklo came over to join them. He looked as though he had just woken up. Percy gave him his present – a white china candlestick with roses round it that the lady in the market had let him have for twenty-five pence as the one that made up the pair was broken.

"It's for you and Wanda for when you get your new trailer," said Percy.

"You're a good sort, you are, son. If you're ever over Slough way, sir," he said, turning to Percy's father, "and you're in need of a good second-hand car, sir, you look me up. I'll see you all right. Thanks son," he said, putting the candlestick carefully down beside him. "Wanda's having a lie down right now, I'll put this by her so she claps 'er eye on it first thing when she wakes. A good little nipper he is, sir. An 'andy bloke to have on the bellows, an' all."

When the tea came, in the ornamental china cups, Lias poured a great splosh of the brandy in each one before handing it round, even in Percy's and Roy's. Roy looked amazed, although it didn't occur to Lias that anything he had done was in any way unusual.

80 "Great!" said Roy out of the side of his mouth

to his brother and the two boys looked anywhere but at their father on the other side of the fire.

Percy finished his delicious peppery tea and went to look for Wingate. He found him straightening the wheel from an old pram with a brick.

Percy gave him a red torch that he had seen lying abandoned in a litter bin in Amesbury.

"Cor, fanks, Perce," he said, examining it expertly.

"It doesn't work very well," Percy apologised. "It's a bit broken."

"That don't matter," said Wingate sportingly. "I'll fix 'im."

81

When Percy joined the others he found that Roy had gone off, at Dicklo's invitation, to look over the horses and Percy's uncle and father were being shown the carved undercarriage of Lias's waggon. The men exchanged glances as they heard laughter from the women coming through the floorboards above their heads.

They had all been enjoying themselves thoroughly for over an hour before Percy's mother appeared at the top of the waggon steps, and, as they walked across the clearing, Lias put his hand on Percy's shoulder.

"I give the old lady your present, son, an' she says them pipe cleaners is just what she always wanted," said Lias. "She won't come down but she said for me to give you this." He gave Percy a small Schweppes bottle full of browny syrup with a screw of newspaper wedged in the neck. "She says for you to take a drop 'afore you goes to sleep an' another drop in the mornin'."

Their goodbyes were said at the edge of the clearing and they were almost out of the wood before Percy realised he still had the present that was meant for Mrs. Doyle, the best present of all — a small brass horseshoe. He ran back and knocked on the waggon door.

It was suffocatingly hot inside. Dim and yellowy and the whole waggon had a strange sickly sweet smell. Mrs. Doyle was washing the tea

cups in a bowl and Lias sat behind her by the
stove. Mrs. Doyle dried her hands on her apron
and while she unwrapped her present, Percy's
eyes wandered around the inside of their home.

The light from a solitary oil lamp picked out
carving and ornamentation everywhere in the
waggon, even across the ceiling and it reflected
in the mirrored doors that closed in front of the
bed. Pushed into the edge of the mirror above
the little stove were curled, old, photographs.
Percy would like to have been shown those, they
were old photographs of horses and people out-

side their waggons. A little bunch of plastic roses was fixed onto the mantelpiece in a wire flower basket.

"That's lovely, son," said Mrs. Doyle, holding up the horseshoe and placing it behind the little rail that ran around the mantelpiece. "That'll look real grand there."

Percy nodded. "I must go now. Goodbye, Mrs. Doyle."

"Goodbye, my son," she said, laying her hand on his head.

He poked his head round the side of Mrs. Doyle's generous figure. "Goodbye Mr. Doyle."

"Bye son," said Lias, lifting his hand in farewell. "Kooshti bok to you, boy."

Percy walked across the clearing to the fire and slowly heaped on more wood. He could hear the rattle of tea cups as Mrs. Doyle finished washing up her china. A dog whined quietly under one of the waggons and Percy had never felt so sad in the whole of his young life. He walked out of the clearing and didn't look back.

Half way down the cart-track he met his uncle coming back to meet him. He took his hand and they walked back to the house in silence.

*   *   *

The next morning was frosty and sunny. To be back in time to greet the visiting grandparents they had had to leave very early.

As they drove along the Amesbury road, brilliantly bathed in early morning sun, Percy saw an ancient dog at the top of the Doyle's lane, following two of the little ones walking barefoot in single file along the grass verge. The taller had an empty bucket over her arm. As they passed, Percy turned and looked through the back window of the landrover. One of the children had left her bucket and gone back to help the other. They both held the old dog by the loose skin at his shoulders and with a child at either side, it was being hauled slithering along the gutter.

"Were they gypsy children?" asked Percy's mother.

Percy's uncle nodded. "Two of them," he said.

His mother turned round in her seat and looked at Percy sitting quietly in the back.

"Don't look so gloomy," she said, putting her finger under his chin and lifting his head. "Mrs. Doyle read my palm, yesterday. She said that we would all meet again."

"Did she?" said Percy. "Did she really? Where?"

"She didn't say where. Mr. Doyle told your father that they go hop-picking every summer at

Halkhurst. If we go to St. Leonards for our holidays again, that's only six miles from Halkhurst. So perhaps you'll see your raggle-taggle gypsies-o in the hop fields next summer."

"Do you think the gypsies might steal him," said Roy. "With a bit of encouragement?"

"You shut up, Roy, or I won't teach you any more Romany words," Percy said furiously.

* * *

Percy stuck his head out of the train window.

"It looks as though you'll be seeing old Lias again, after all . . ." said his uncle. "You're off, now." He walked along beside the train as it began to move away.

"If Mrs. Doyle says we will," said Percy, "then I bet we will."

He pushed his arm through the window and kept waving to the solitary figure on the platform as it got smaller and smaller.

"Kooshti bok, Uncle," he called back, "Kooshti bok."